T0146778

Once Upon a Time...

SPIRITUAL FAIRY TALES

PATRIZIA PALENZONA

BALBOA.
PRESS
A DIVISION OF HAY HOUSE

Balboa Press books may be ordered through booksellers or by contacting:

Balboa Press
A Division of Hay House
1663 Liberty Drive
Bloomington, IN 47403
www.balboapress.com
1 (877) 407-4847

Because of the dynamic nature of the Internet, any web addresses or links contained in this book may have changed since publication and may no longer be valid. The views expressed in this work are solely those of the author and do not necessarily reflect the views of the publisher, and the publisher hereby disclaims any responsibility for them.

The author of this book does not dispense medical advice or prescribe the use of any technique as a form of treatment for physical, emotional, or medical problems without the advice of a physician, either directly or indirectly. The intent of the author is only to offer information of a general nature to help you in your quest for emotional and spiritual well-being. In the event you use any of the information in this book for yourself, which is your constitutional right, the author and the publisher assume no responsibility for your actions.

Any people depicted in stock imagery provided by Thinkstock are models, and such images are being used for illustrative purposes only.
Certain stock imagery © Thinkstock.

Print information available on the last page.

ISBN: 978-1-5043-2783-1 (sc)
ISBN: 978-1-5043-2785-5 (hc)
ISBN: 978-1-5043-2784-8 (e)

Library of Congress Control Number: 2015902334

Balboa Press rev. date: 02/24/2015

Contents

Things Are Not Always What They Appear to Be

*O*nce upon a time, in a small, ancient village, there lived an orphan boy. He never got to know his mother, as she had passed away while giving birth to him six years ago. His father, who was a hardworking man, had managed to take care of him lovingly, but one day he became very sick. The doctor came and, after examining his father for a long time, explained to the boy that they had to take him to the hospital in the nearby village. The boy was terrified, as he had never been alone before, but all his pleading to leave his father with him was in vain. His father hugged him tightly, his eyes full of tears. Then two big men came into their little cottage and, with the doctor's help, led his father to a carriage that was waiting outside.

This was the last time he saw his father.

So the boy was given to an elderly man and his wife who lived close by and who had no children of their own. With time, he became very fond of them, and they loved him as their own son. He was a very shy child and liked to keep to himself.

He loved to explore the streets of their village, which was set on a hill. There he would roam through the narrow roads and climb up stairs that were leading to other small roads. The village was filled with hidden spaces waiting to be discovered.

One late afternoon, while the sun was setting, the boy was walking toward a section of the village he had never been to before. Suddenly, something caught his attention. There was an object on the ground that glistened as if made by light. Excitedly, he got closer, and as he bent down, he saw it was a small card.

He picked it up, curious to see what treasure he had found. But all of a sudden, the glitter was gone. On the front of the card, he could see the design of a red, velvet curtain, just like in theaters, pulled back against a black background. On it, written in gold, was "Things are not always what they appear to be."

Again, the card started to glisten. The boy was amazed and fascinated by what he saw, for the card appeared to have a life of its own. He carefully turned it around and saw the design of an eye in the middle of a triangle. "What is this all about?" he asked himself aloud. On the bottom of the triangle was "Harvest Road number 17."

Without further delay, he started walking, determined to find that road. He asked around, but no one seemed to know for sure where it was.

That night, he returned home, deciding not to mention anything about his finding to anyone. Early the next morning, he went again in search of the road. He had to find out more about this mysterious, scintillating card with the name of a street nobody knew.

On the third day, after wandering around with no results and feeling disheartened, he sat near a fountain and took the card out of his pocket one more time. To his surprise, it started glistening again. *What a mysterious card it is,* he thought. He raised his eyes and his glance fell upon a pole that he had not noticed before. On top of the pole was a sign on which was written the name of a street. Excitedly, he checked with his card, but to his dismay, it was not the name he was searching for. *Oh God, help,* he thought, feeling more and more discouraged.

Again, he looked at the sign on the pole, feeling so disappointed that he wanted to give up his search. He could not believe his eyes. All of a sudden, the sign started to scintillate and glisten, revealing in lights "Harvest Road." It just lasted for a moment, and then it returned to the ordinary street sign with the former name.

The boy could not believe what was going on, but more than ever, he was captivated by what was happening. Full of newly gained energy, he started walking up the narrow road, in search of the number 17.

The dusty road wound around old houses, some so old that they had no numbers at all, as weather and time had erased any mark there would have been many years ago. It was already getting late in the evening, and it was hard for him to see. Still, not too far away, he spotted a small shop. As he was searching its walls for a number, his heart stopped a beat. For a split second, he saw, in the most magnificent scintillating colors, the number 17. His excitement grew and, with a fast-beating heart, he went to the front door; finally, he had found the house he was looking for.

But the door was locked, with a sign that read, "Closed For The Season."

He peaked inside the window and saw shelves filled with beautiful bottles of different sizes and colors, and one of the signs read, "Gem Elixirs." On the other side of the store, he saw other sets of beautiful bottles with a sign saying, "Teas For The Soul."

The boy was thrilled! He had found the place. He had never seen it before, and he could not wait until it would open its doors, although he was not sure when that would be.

From then on, every evening he would go to the store and peak inside the window. He felt a magical presence emanating from the place, but he always found its doors closed.

Many weeks passed until one evening, as he was approaching the store, he suddenly stopped. He could hear delightful music and saw light coming from the windows.

He walked slowly toward the house. As he got closer, he could see that the store was filled with people who were beautifully dressed, sitting around a big table. It seemed like they were talking joyfully, and it appeared that they were drinking something out of cups. They all seemed very happy.

The boy didn't dare get too close. Still, he was able to see that there was one empty chair at the table. While he was standing bewildered outside the house, still marveling at the scene inside, the entry door to the shop opened silently and a pathway started to glisten, from the door all the way toward his feet. He was speechless, but some inner force made him walk toward the store. He felt as if an invisible hand guided him.

As he entered shyly, the beautiful people, who looked as if they were from another world, stopped talking, and the eldest person addressed the boy. "Welcome, young man. We were waiting for you," he said. "Please sit down and join us, for there is something we would like to speak to you about."

The boy carefully sat at the edge of the empty chair and was offered some tea in a cup. "We invite you to drink this tea, which will fill you with knowledge."

The man continued to address the boy. "Your presence on earth is very important at this time, and as you grow, you will greatly influence the people in your village and the neighboring lands. Just remember, things in life are not always what they appear to be."

With that, he lifted his finger and traced a luminous screen that appeared before everyone's eyes.

On the screen, the boy could see the life of a woman who barely had means to sustain herself and her child. Everyone at the table was a witness to all the hardships she had gone through in life in order to nourish her child and herself.

The master of the ceremony explained, "All the hardship this woman has gone through has made her very strong inside, though she was born weak in character. During her life, she has developed the strength of a warrior. She has been transformed in such a way that nothing will stop her from following her path."

Transfixed, the boy watched what was shown to him.

Once again, the master lifted his finger, and everyone saw on the screen the lives of two young men. They were friends who were looking for means to sustain their lives. One position was offered at the baker's shop, and they were both asked to speak with the owner, to inform him about their skills.

The first of the friends told the baker all the great tasks he could accomplish, exaggerating in ways that were far from the truth. The second friend had been very honest with the baker, also telling him about his talents, which were many, but staying humble and within the truth.

The next day, both of the boys were called before the baker to hear his decision regarding which one he would give the work to. To the surprise of both friends, the job was given to the first contestant, the one who had not spoken the truth, for the baker was impressed by his abilities and believed in him.

The second friend left feeling heartbroken. In the beginning, he felt pain inside, then he felt frustration and slowly anger started swelling up. *Why is life so unjust? Why is honesty not recognized?* After that, he did not see his friend for a long time. But very often, he would think about him. They had been friends since childhood, and he was unhappy that they could no longer trust each other.

As time passed, his tolerance grew deeper; he began to understand that his friend had acted from a place of ignorance and emptiness within. His anger turned into compassion. And as he started to recognize his friend's behavior, he started to forgive him. He felt at peace with himself, and he again experienced the love for his friend that had been missing all this time.

Not long thereafter, he found the perfect occupation for himself, which let him live more comfortably and happily than he could have ever imagined.

The master of ceremony explained, "When one's life seems to be filled with great injustice, it is demonstrating what you need to work upon, in order to develop virtue inside you." He then continued to show the lives of many people, displaying all types of situations.

The boy, as young as he was, came to understand that there is no wrong in life. Everything that happens is good for us, beneficial for our own growth. And if things do not appear to be that way, we just need to take a closer look, widen our perspectives, and see what needs to be worked upon inside, in order to bring good into our lives.

Just as the master had predicted, the boy grew to be a great man who helped transform the lives of many people in the neighboring lands, bringing back peace and love into their hearts and souls.

The Doctor and His Wife

*O*nce upon a time, there was a beautiful little valley where it was springtime all year round. Trees and plants would bloom abundantly, and everyone in the village lived happily doing their daily chores.

In this village lived a handsome young doctor. Everyone loved him, as whenever he was needed, he was quick to help.

It so happened that his father was a great and wise man, one who knew that the real healing elements were to be found in nature. He knew every plant, every grass and every flower. He would spend hours in the meadows collecting whatever was needed to make of it a healing remedy.

The young doctor, who was then a small boy, loved to accompany his father, and as time went by, he learned to recognize those plants that had healing powers. Many a times, one could see the father and his son leaving the village, carrying a sack on their shoulders, going in search of the rare plants, which were found in the nearby meadows. When they returned in the late afternoon, they would sit together in their small kitchen and lovingly and with great respect sort the plants into big earthen containers that were labeled with the names of the plants. His father told him that they were holding great treasures that, if combined in the right way, could heal many human ailments. Day by day, the little boy learned from his father how to collect, prepare, and extract the healing powers from the many flowers and plants that they found so generously in the valley.

Time passed by and the little boy had become a handsome man of many virtues. He knew all the secrets of the plants, and every so often, people would come to him for remedies when they felt sick.

One day his aging father called him to his side and said, "My dear son, you have learned all the potencies of the plants. You have learned to combine them and to use them well. As my days are coming to an end, I will impart to you the most important of all the healing secrets. You not only must heal the body; you also must heal the soul."

With these words, he closed his eyes.

People came from far and near to be treated by the young doctor who could heal in miraculous ways. Whatever their sickness was, he would prepare a special tea, using the herbs he had collected in the meadows, and their ailments would be healed. This was what people would see on the surface, but his treatment was much deeper. It would reach profound levels of one's being that were invisible to the eye. The doctor treated each person with love, understanding, and simplicity. But he still kept the secret his father had revealed to him.

The doctor kept working in this way, when one day he met a beautiful girl. Her eyes radiated pure light, and her smile brought great joy to his heart. They loved each other dearly, and not much time passed before they were married. Their lives were full of happiness and harmony.

The young woman helped her husband collect the plants in the meadows and sort them into the earthen pots, just as he had done with his father so many years before. It was a simple life, but one filled with love and gratitude. Each night they would give thanks together to their Creator for all their blessings, but most of all for the opportunity to help other people. That was what brought great happiness to their hearts.

One morning, as they were awakening from their sleep, the doctor looked at his dear wife and noticed that the light in her eyes had begun to fade. As days went by, she became very ill. All of a sudden, it seemed as if her whole life was fading away.

The doctor went to the meadows; he knew exactly which plants he was looking for. He needed them fresh so they would contain all their life force.

As soon as he was back at their home, he started to prepare his special tea and began his treatment. He said to his wife, "This tea is infused with the life force of the universe. Drink it slowly and listen carefully. Know that you are deeply loved by those you can see and by those you cannot see. Feel the love pulsating inside of you. You must let go of any and all attachments, including me. This will free you from the bonds that tie you to fear. Find any reason to be happy. Guide your mind gently, and it will follow. Stay anchored in this state. Happiness releases chemicals in the body that can outgrow any sickness found on earth. Grow from it and become strong—so strong that there will be nothing in this world that will take away this light in your eyes."

As the wife kept sipping her tea and listening to her doctor, her beloved husband, she began to feel better and better, while the doctor's words resonated within every cell of her being.

Days passed by, and the doctor's wife was feeling stronger and stronger; her eyes were shining bright. She had learned to master her sickness and became a blazing light for all to see.

The young doctor rested in great happiness. He had imparted his secret with his dear love, and together they became of service to all the people in need.

The Bakers

*O*nce upon a time, in the ancient days, there was a village renowned for having the best cooks and bakers. However, it had not always been that way, for the cooks had received very special training throughout the years, which began with one young man. He had become the organizer of a special event that took place once a year in the village's fair. While he was preparing for this year's event, his mind drifted back, many years ago, to when he was a small, six-year-old boy.

He lived with his parents on the outskirts of the village. They were so poor that they could not afford to live where all the other villagers stayed, so his father had built a small hut right besides the woods. Every morning his father would get up early, gather his ax and tools and leave to chop wood. Later on, his mother would join him.

She went looking for berries and mushrooms, herbs and roots, which they would take to the village and sell in the market.

In the meantime, he waited for them at home. His mother had taught him how to attend the little vegetable garden, which she had planted behind the cottage. There he loved to spend his days while waiting for his parents. He would weed the garden, and he watched fascinated when he saw the first sprouts of vegetable making their way through the earth. He would spend hours in the little garden, giving water when needed and protecting the tender plants when a storm was too strong. In this way, he came to love all that the earth would offer them so generously.

His mother also had taught him how to use the vegetables, and already at his early age, he was able to make some dishes that, when his parents came back from the woods, they would enjoy together. His mother would praise him, for everything he cooked was delicious and full of flavor. Indeed, it seemed that all the love his little heart felt for his plants, he would pour into the dishes that he put before his parents.

Always before eating, when they sat around their simple table, his father would say a prayer, thanking God for their food and for their good fortune to be able to live such a healthy and blessed live. They were a happy family, full of simplicity and love for each other.

Once every year, in the bigger village nearby, there was a fair. It lasted for seven days, and people would come from all the neighboring villages. It was a big event, and grownups as well as children would wait anxiously for it to take place.

His father and his mother would take him, just for one day, as they could not afford to neglect their daily chores of collecting the wood and berries. It was during this time of the year when they would sell the most to the market, as there were also many stands of food at the fair.

The night before the fair, when he was already in bed, he remembered seeing his mother, sitting beside their oil lamp, sowing and patching his only pair of long pants.

They were the same ones he had used the year before, so she had to make them longer, as he had already outgrown them. Also, his father's shirt needed some mending, and his mother was still sitting by the lamp, when he fell asleep, happily dreaming about the fair the next day.

Early in the morning, his mother dressed him in his finest clothes, making sure his pants fit properly. Then she checked on her husband. She herself looked as beautiful as he had ever seen her. Her thick, brown hair was pulled back into a bun, and her pale-blue dress matched her lovely eyes.

They walked for more than one hour to get to the fair. Holding his parents' hands, his heart beat excitedly as they got closer. They could already hear the music from far away, and as they came closer, they could make out the voices of children calling out in delight.

They passed through the entry and saw the most beautiful and colorful tents one could imagine. He pulled his father's hand in excitement.

Through an opening on one of the tents, he saw an old woman sitting on a chair, surrounded by children. She had just begun to tell a story of a king and queen living in a beautiful castle high atop a mountain. In her story, glittering snow fell upon the castle and deer grazed close by. The lady had such a magical way of telling the story, he was already lost in her fantasy when the tent keeper came and closed the gap he had been looking through, for his parents had not the money to pay for the entrance.

They kept on walking and came upon a tent where pure magic was taking place. The door was open, and he could see the most extraordinary things. Frightened, he watched as a magician cut one woman right through the middle of her body. He remembered squeezing his father's hand tightly; his eyes wide open in disbelief.

Then they got lucky. They came to a tent with marionettes, and his father knew the doorkeeper so all three of them got a place in the last row.

What a delight! It was the happiest day of his life. He never had seen so many miraculous things, all in one day.

But now, after they were so fortunate to see the whole show of the marionettes, came the best part of the day. His father had saved some money to buy for his wife and son sweets from the bakers. Each one was allowed to choose exactly what they wanted. For a long time, they walked around, looking at all the delicacies that were displayed so beautifully. Finally, after thinking it over for a long time, he decided on a small, heart-shaped chocolate cake. It was decorated with white icing and topped with a little paper umbrella in the most beautiful pink he could imagine. His mother got a huge white cookie, which she shared with her husband. They found a bench and all three of them sat down, enjoying with gratitude in their hearts those fine foods.

It was getting late, so they took one last walk around the colorful and magical fair, and then they started, hand in hand, their long journey back home.

What an extraordinary day it had been. When he lay in bed that night, he wished with all his heart that one day he would be able to bake such fine delicacies as he had seen in the fair.

Lost in memory, the organizer of the fair fixed tables and benches for the event that night. He set up eight tables, which were designated for the eight young adults to whom he would teach his baking skills. Each baking station had its own stove. Carefully, he put fine ingredients for each of the youngsters on their tables. Then he checked on the benches where the spectators would sit, as a lot of people came to watch the cooking lessons.

His mind began again to drift back, this time to when he was eleven years of age. By now, he was already experienced in cooking a variety of foods, but what he liked the most was when his mother would bring home some eggs, flour, and sugar, which she had traded at the market for berries or mushrooms, and he could try to bake some cakes and cookies. He would spend a lot of time carefully thinking how to best use the ingredients, and when his parents came home at night, they would taste the most delicious cake they had ever tasted. As young as he still was, he had already become a baker with extraordinary talents.

It was again time for the annual fair. His father and mother had gone early into the woods while he stayed at home. As his parents could not take him to the fair this year, he baked for them one of his special cakes.

Softly, he hummed a melody while preparing and mixing those precious ingredients that would be transformed into a most delightful cake.

He had just put the pan in the oven when he heard a knock on the door. Surprised, he went to see, as they never had any visitors.

He was astonished to find a young, tall man at the doorsteps. He radiated a love and warmth, which he could feel immediately. He remembered not being scared at all; it felt as if he had known this visitor for a long time. He asked the young man inside and offered him a seat, while he stood looking at him inquisitively.

The mysterious young man spoke to him. "I know that your wish for many years has been to bake for the annual fair in the nearby village. You will go to the fair and bake their cakes and delicacies and teach the bakers of the village your secrets. Go tomorrow, early in the morning. You will find a place where you can bake. You also will find all the ingredients you need."

With that, the visitor smiled at him, got up from his chair, and walked out the door. When he went to the door to look once more at the strange and beautiful visitor, he was nowhere to be seen.

He could not wait for his parents to return, to tell them what had happened. As they all ate the delicious cake he had baked that night, his father prayed again, thanking for all their blessings, and asking for the protection of his boy, whom he would take to the fair the next morning.

He still remembered when they set out early the next day, starting their long walk to the fair, not really knowing what to expect or where to go. When they entered the fair, they walked toward the food stands when, from a little distance away, they could hear a big commotion going on. People were running around nervously, throwing up their hands in the air in disbelief. They were moving around ingredients of food, taking pans here and there, checking on their ovens, and really not knowing what to do.

When he and his father approached, they inquired what was going on. They were told that the head baker, who was not only going to bake but, as a special treat, was also giving baking instructions to the youngsters, had fallen ill and could not come. There was already a crowd of young people sitting on benches that had been placed in the square for this special event, waiting in anticipation for the head baker to start his lessons. His father looked at him, and they knew what to do. Together, they walked up to one of the men who seemed to be in charge, and his father told him proudly of his young son's talents.

Again, the young organizer checked all the stations; evening was approaching and the oil lamps were burning. The spectators were already seated when, one by one, the participants came in, taking their places at each station. When the organizer saw that everybody was ready, he spoke. "I salute each one of you on this evening. My wish is that all of you, as well as the spectators, will learn from this event today. You have all the finest ingredients before you, and you will be able to make the most delectable and exquisite dishes. I wish to share with you my secrets today."

He looked around and then continued. "I have been cooking and baking since I was a small child. When I was still very young, I learned how to respect and appreciate each one of the foods the earth gives us. I learned that the vegetables, fruits, and roots are living substances that can nourish us in a way far beyond our understanding. They can vitalize us if needed, and they can calm us if used in a different way. Food is vital for every human being. It is filled with energy, which sustains our body.

"Never forget, food is a gift from the earth to us. Respect it as such, and love it with this understanding. Bear in mind, when preparing your food, that it is the feelings you have toward the food and the way you cook it that makes all the difference between one dish and another. Anything you do with love will be transformed in magical ways.

"I was fortunate to have learned this at an early age. When I saw my parents going off to the woods each morning, despite the rigorous and tiring work the forest demanded of them, they always left happy and in good spirits. And when they returned, they were always cheerful and in good moods. There was serenity about their fate and their jobs, which in turn always made me happy.

"Despite the circumstances, they had a true love and passion for what they did. And as years went by, I slowly began to learn and understand the meaning and purpose of love in a person's work. And how, when anything is done with true love in one's heart, the outcome is always better, tastier, happier, and more perfect.

"Know that your thoughts and feelings are energy that get into the food you prepare and consequentially will get absorbed by the person who tastes it. Always keep this in mind when preparing your dishes.

"And now, please begin."

A delightful music started to play in the background as the young adults began to bake. The organizer watched with delight, as he could sense that each and every one of the young contestants took his words to heart. He could feel their love for preparing this fine food. He gave them all the time they needed, and when he saw that the last one took his food out from the oven, he rang a gong.

Then he spoke again. "I can see you have done well. You respected the ingredients and cooked with love. Please bring your delicacies to be tasted, by all of our guests as well as by all of you.

"Tonight I have shared with you a very special secret. It is not so much what you choose to cook; it is all about the love and feelings you put into your dishes as you prepare them. Every person tasting your food will be satisfied and will benefit in a perfect way."

And so it was that the fair became the most popular in all the country. It was renowned for its delicious foods. No one really knew what it was that made this food so special, but the cooks had developed the ability to prepare the finest meals that would affect, in a magical way, anyone who would consume them.

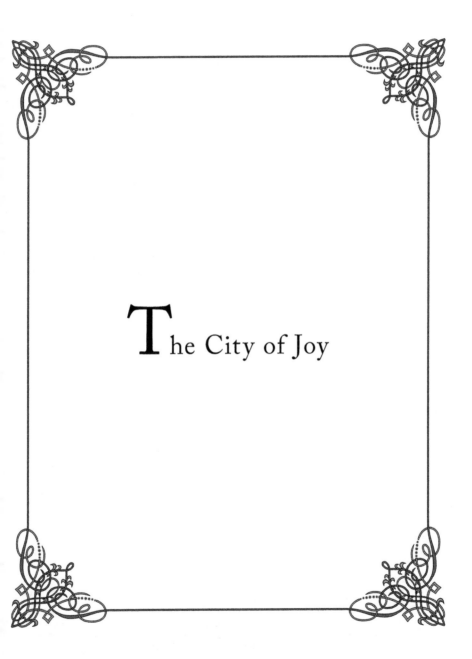

The City of Joy

*O*nce upon a time, there was a very small village that had exquisite gardens adorned with the most beautiful flowers that emanated their divine fragrance. In this village, people lived their lives merrily and happily. They had an understanding of life that went beyond the ordinary. Every day was a celebration for them. Also, if on occasions things did not appear to go smoothly, they celebrated, for they knew there was a lesson to be learned and they were looking forward to the transformation it would bring.

In the village, there lived a young man who decided one day to go out and venture into the neighboring lands. "I will be back in a few days," he told his parents.

That evening they celebrated at home, and with the blessings of his parents he went off on his horse the following day.

After three days of travel, as evening was approaching, he arrived at the neighboring village. He decided to stay at an inn, where he could get food and shelter and his horse could rest and be nourished as well. After a hot supper, he felt eager to explore his surroundings, so he went out for a walk on the streets of the village.

He saw many people gathered and a parade seemed to be passing by. He was surprised when he saw people with solemn faces walking down the street. Behind them, six men were carrying on top of their shoulders a big box that seemed to be heavy. Following was a group of people with tears running down their faces. They appeared to be very sad. What a strange vision this was for the young man.

He asked someone in the crowd what was going on.

"The tailor has passed away," he was told, "and his family is mourning his death."

The young man didn't say anything but thought this to be very peculiar. Why were they crying? Why were they so sad? He went back to the inn for a good night's rest.

The following day, he inquired a little more about the customs of the people in the village with the innkeeper. He learned that it was a village with hardworking people. Oftentimes, their life was difficult and they struggled to provide food for their families. For that reason, many people became worried and unhappy. And if bad fortune came upon them and somebody died, they mourned for a long time, as they did not always understand the injustices of life.

The young man listened surprised, as all this was very new to him.

As he prepared for his departure, he told the innkeeper, of whom he had become fond in such a short time, "Maybe someday you would like to visit our village."

And so he started his way back, having made a new friend and having learned about customs of other places.

At the end of the third day, when he arrived at his home, he was greeted with cheer and love. "Tell us about your travel," his parents encouraged their son.

"The strangest thing happened," he said. And then he began to tell them about what he had seen.

They all celebrated the blessing to live the life they had.

A few months went by and, one day as the young man was walking down the street, to his surprise, he encountered the innkeeper from the neighboring village.

"My brother is taking care of the inn for a few days and I have come to visit your village," the innkeeper said.

The young man invited his friend for lunch to celebrate their encounter. He took the innkeeper to a beautiful little tavern where they found a table in the shade under a big tree. They ate a simple but delicious meal, while the innkeeper told his young friend all about his three days of travel. Then he said, "I came to your village to meet your people and to learn of your customs."

The young man remembered when he had visited the innkeeper's village. He felt great compassion in his heart, and he began to explain. "Our whole life is a celebration. When one passes away, one is not bound to the earth anymore. We rejoice in the new journey of the soul for that person, for we know that the soul is free to travel anywhere it wishes to. We have developed in our village the ability to see with the inner eye and to hear with the inner ear. Anytime we would like to see our beloved, departed ones we call them with our minds, and by doing so, they do appear and talk to us if there would be the need.

"We are also aware that departed souls have a period in which they need to rest, and by calling on to them too often, we would be disturbing this period of rest for them. Furthermore, departed souls have their duties as well once they leave life on earth, and we do respect that too.

"At the time of their departure, we offer their used bodies into a flame, with fragrant incense and resins, and the ashes are used to cultivate the most beautiful gardens, which are filled with blossoming flowers.

"We do celebrate their departure from the physical body into the light of God, and we do celebrate with joy. For we can see them as happy, wonderful beings of light who rejoice in this state of freedom."

As strange as all this was for the innkeeper to hear, something was resonating in the depths of his being.

The young man continued. "Energy is contagious by nature. If you are in the company of people who do not feel well within themselves, you will start to feel ill at ease. In the same way, if you are in the company of people who are happy by nature, you will start to feel better and better yourself.

"In this village, we know, and we are aware of the one responsibility we have in life. Each person that we come in contact with in our lives is in contact with our attitude. Our attitude is energy, and that energy is contagious. We all have the power to make people feel happier and better within themselves."

The innkeeper was indeed feeling the energy of joy in the air. He did not say anything for a long time, as he started to feel happier and happier.

The young man, sensing the innkeeper's wishes, invited him to move with his family into his village.

And so it was that time went by. The village became a town, and the town became a city. A city known as … The City of Joy.

The Two Brothers

*O*nce upon a time, in a beautiful kingdom, where the land blessed its people with bountiful harvests, there lived a king and queen who were loved by all. The king ruled his land with great care and the queen made sure that all their people lived happily. Time passed in great harmony and, over the years, two sons were born.

The first son was born blind, while the second son, who was one year younger, had strong vitality and health. Both brothers were born with a noble heart. They got along very well with each other, the younger boy always helping out his older brother. Their days were filled with play and laughter, and when the older brother was in need, the younger one was quick by his side. In this way, they spent their childhood happy and safe, in the kingdom of their parents.

For generations, it had been a custom for the eldest child to inherit the throne. But in this case, as the eldest one was blind, everyone agreed, including both brothers, that the younger son would better accomplish the royal duties. And so it was decided that he should be the king's successor.

As the two brothers became young adults, the blind one developed a quality that went beyond the senses. He became very keen at recognizing the energy of the people around him, and he started to feel their true intentions.

By this time, the king had made it his habit to always invite his two sons to any negotiation taking place in the palace. He gave great importance to the advice of his older son, as many times he proved to be right.

As the young man was not able to see the outside world, he began to focus all his attention inside, and something mysterious started to happen. At first, he began to sense the energy of the objects around him, feeling their heat when he got close to them. Over time, the energy transformed itself into particles of light and took on the form of the objects. Before he knew it, he could see all there was around him with his inner eye. His family was amazed that he no longer needed help to move around. Nobody could explain what kind of miracle was taking place.

What nobody knew was that every night when he went to bed, an angel came to visit him. He would sit beside his bed, speaking softly. He would teach him how to use his inner vision and how to rely on his senses. The youngster waited in anticipation for these nightly visits for they made him very happy, and he felt immense gratitude toward his angel. He would always listen carefully to the instruction he received, and then gently drift into sleep. When he awoke the next morning, he eagerly put into practice what he had been taught the night before, as he always remembered well the instructions imparted by the angel.

As time went by, it was the older son who started helping his younger brother and his parents, teaching them how to become more sensitive to the inner world. They would appreciate this very much for they could see how it changed their perception of their daily lives. They were learning how not only to judge with their minds, but more importantly, with their hearts. It was a long and sweet learning process, each one becoming more and more kindhearted and understanding of themselves and their fellow men.

And so the years went by.

As the king got older, the appointed date for his succession and the coronation of his younger son to inherit the throne approached. The entire kingdom started preparing for this magnificent event and the festivities to follow. Excitement filled the air!

The grand day arrived and the royal family prepared to go to the court, where the coronation was to take place. A big tribune had been built, decorated with ribbons and flowers, and many chairs were placed in front for all their invited guests.

The royal family sat on the beautiful seats that had been handcrafted for this important occasion, and the king, making sure that all guests were comfortable and seated, started to deliver his speech. He told all his people how much he loved his sons and how important their decisions and understanding had become for him over the years. He emphasized how his sons had learned to respect and love their kingdom and how they were prepared to take good care of its people.

He further explained that it had been decided for his younger son to be his successor, in view of the impaired vision of the older one. As the king was finishing his speech, and the crown was handed to him, the younger son asked for permission to speak.

"My dear father, mother, and citizens of this beautiful kingdom, I am grateful for this tremendous honor that is being bestowed upon me. I am sure I would do my very best to become a great king, but my conscience would not rest if I were to accept this great honor.

"My brother may not be able to see like the rest of us, but of one thing be assured. His vision is far greater than ours, for he can not only see perfectly every object with his inner eyes, but he can also see what lies beyond the surface of things, people, and events.

"He is far better qualified then I am to rule this kingdom, and I ask that the crown be placed on his head."

There was not one dry eye in the crowd, and everyone started cheering and applauding. The king, who knew his youngest son had spoken the truth and was moved beyond tears with emotion, placed the crown on the head of his older son.

At that moment, he told his older son that he always knew he had been the chosen one to lead the kingdom into a new era. He had also known that he had to step aside and let his younger son make that decision.

From that day on, the new king followed the steps of his father and brought the kingdom into an age of wealth and prosperity to levels never seen before. He was loved by all and became known through the ages as the king who could see with no eyes.

The Master and the Disciple

*O*nce upon a time on a high mountaintop, there was a sage who lived in an old hut. He had five disciples who stayed nearby. They all wanted to learn as much as they could from the master's wisdom.

One of the disciples was of small stature. He had been with the master the longest. When he was four years of age, both of his parents had died of a disease that was ravaging the village where they lived. The boy, who had survived, was handed from one relative to the next, when finally he stayed for some years with his aunt, the sister of his father. She was not married and was happy to have someone who could help her as she worked in the fields. She was a good woman, and together, they made life more bearable for each other.

It so happened that his aunt was a great devotee of the sage who lived in the forest, a day's journey away. Once a year, she would go to pay her respects to the master, and on those occasions, she would take him along with her. When the young boy was ten years of age, his aunt became very sick and weak, and the master, hearing of her condition, invited him to stay with him in his hut in the woods. The boy accepted gladly, as he had already become very fond of the master.

He would clean the master's hut, venture into the woods to find some eatables, make a fire, and cook. He made sure to take care of his master in any way he could.

Every day at sunrise, the other four disciples would arrive one by one. The young boy made tea for them all, then he would sit in the back of the room, listening to the teachings and the great wisdom the master would share with them. He always treasured those moments; his heart would open wide, and he would feel an overwhelming love for his master.

But over time, every so often during those precious morning hours, while the other four disciples would be sipping their tea waiting for their master to impart his wisdom onto them, the master would ask him to do some errands. He commanded him to go to the village and fetch some more tea and sugar. Other times, he would send him to the washer man to take his clothes, or he would ask him to go to the market to get some milk. The boy would carry out all his duties the best he could, but with a heavy heart. He loved his master more than anything else and would do whatever he could to please him. Nonetheless, whenever he was sent away, he felt hurt, rejected, and unloved.

In the meantime, the master gave all his attention on the other four disciples. They were always happy to see the small boy leave. They wondered why the master would waste time with the boy, who was still young of age and with no understanding whatsoever. They were proud of themselves that they could learn so quickly and were competing for their master's attention. They would do anything to become more relevant and important before his eyes.

When the boy would come back after the long walk up the mountain, having accomplished his master's wishes, the other disciples were usually all gone, as the morning sessions were over. Although disappointed, the boy was also happy to have the master all to himself again. He would pour all his love out to him, anticipating all the master's wishes and fulfilling them readily.

But to the boy's dismay, the master's behavior toward him did not change. When he was not sending him away, he would completely ignore him. The boy would sit unnoticed in the back of the room while the other disciples took notes and interacted with the master in animated ways.

At that time, he started questioning himself. What did he do wrong? Why had the master stopped loving him? He became very sad and depressed, but the more miserable he felt, the more he started focusing inside of himself and on his own feelings.

What was this all about? He had devoted so many years serving his master, loving him beyond anything, and now he would not even get a glance from him? He felt very unhappy and looked for ways to change that.

Slowly, he started to nurture his own heart, loving himself and expanding the energy within. He continued doing his service devotedly, but now his focus was more on his work and on the love he could put into it. As he lived this way, he noticed that all of a sudden it didn't matter anymore which one of the disciples the master favored. And when he was sent away, he felt calm and happy just as well. From then on, his days were filled with gratitude and love.

Years passed and one day the master called upon the boy, who had become a young adult. "I have been observing you all this time. Even when you thought I was not watching or paying attention to you. I want you to know you are and have always been my dearest disciple."

Tears of love welled in the boy's eyes.

The master continued. "In the beginning, your energy was scattered and your love was overflowing; it was completely directed toward me, making you forget about yourself. Now, after many years, I can say you have learned to contain your love. You have made it grow within yourself. When it is contained in this way, it becomes more strong and powerful. Today I can say you are no longer my student."

The young man, who did not understand, looked quietly at his master, so the sage continued. "You have learned to conquer your own feelings and your own mind. Today I can say you have become a master."

From that day on, the master and his disciple lived their days as two beloved brothers, and that conversation remained their most guarded secret.

The Forest

*O*nce upon a time, there was a deep, vast forest. It was said to have enchanting and magical properties. People came from near and far to experience the magic it was so well known for. But for most of them, the forest was not magical at all and when they returned home there was not much to tell their families, except maybe how they had defended themselves from some wild animal. So the forest, through the ages, had become a mysterious place feared by some and worshiped by others.

The nearest village was at a six-day walking distance. In it lived a righteous young man. Since when he was a small boy, his grandfather had spoken to him about the magnificence of the forest. Many times, he asked his grandfather to tell him more about it, but for some strange reason, his grandfather had not been able to.

One night, the young man had a dream in which he found himself deep inside the forest. He was sitting under a tree, leaning against its enormous trunk with his eyes closed, when all of a sudden he heard a voice calling out his name. He got up and looked around but could not see anyone. He started to walk and came to a lake of indescribable beauty. He was drawn to it, and just as he was going to step inside, his dream ended and he woke up.

As he thought about his dream, he felt that the time had come to explore the forest for himself. So the next morning, he made all the arrangements to embark on the journey, taking with him a satchel with only a few provisions that could nourish him in time of need. He started his walk toward the meadows, wondering if the forest would reveal to him its magic.

At the end of the sixth day, as the sun was beginning to set, he finally reached the outskirts of the beautiful forest. As he came closer, he could feel that he was entering a sacred place. The trees emanated some kind of rarefied oxygen that began to nurture every cell of his being.

He walked for some distance when, to his surprise, he noticed that he was not hungry anymore. He was being completely nourished by the air and did not feel the need for food. He left his satchel behind and kept on his way.

The temperature had adjusted itself, where he no longer felt hot or cold.

It had grown dark by now, but the moonlight was showing him all there was to see. Somehow, any fatigue he felt had completely melted away, replaced with a kind of energy that was subtle yet powerful, which he had never felt before. The moonlight guided his way into an opening where he saw the most beautiful lake mirroring its surroundings with a silvery hue.

He sat underneath a tree, rejoicing in the beautiful scenery. At that moment, he heard an owl calling out. He closed his eyes, taking in the sounds of the forest, when suddenly he heard a rustling in the bushes. And before he could look around, he saw a big bear standing in front of him. For some reason he was not afraid. He felt protected, in a way he could not describe. He kept very still, transmitting to the bear that he meant no harm. The bear seemed to sense his energy and slowly walked away.

The young man kept sitting there, and soon the most exquisite incense he had ever smelled enveloped him. Where was this coming from? He could not see anyone around him.

Once again, the owl was calling.

Just as he began wondering if there was any explanation to all he experienced, he heard a gallop in the distance. The sound got closer and louder, and soon he could see two white horses. They stopped a short distance away, just in time for him to see how beautiful they were, their long mane almost touching the ground. One of the horses made the sound of a snort, as if calling out to him, and then suddenly both horses went off, disappearing into the fog.

Not long after, he was still pondering about this marvelous place he had encountered when he heard the gallop once again. As the horses came closer, they stopped a little distance away from him and again one of the horses made the snorting sound. This time, the young man got up and started walking very gently toward the horses. Both of them kept very still, encouraging him to get closer.

He sensed that they wanted to take him somewhere, when one of the horses lowered its head, inviting him to get on its back. He carefully mounted the horse while holding onto its long mane, and both horses started to gallop, his horse leading the way.

When the pathway grew wider, revealing they were getting close to a vast meadow, he could hear that the other horse was passing him. But to his surprise, when he turned back he saw a man of extraordinary features riding the other horse. The man looked straight into his eyes, with a smile on his face, but did not say anything. He passed the young man, his garments floating in the air. Where had he come from? Instinctively, the young man knew that this extraordinary being must belong to the magical forest. The horses galloped through the meadows, one behind the other. They jumped over branches and obstacles as if they were flying away.

An indescribable joy began to overwhelm the young man's entire being; he had never felt like this before. The horses continued their gallop, until they reached the other side of the meadow, then they slowed down to a walk, entering once again the forest. Not a word was spoken.

Finally, the horses stopped in front of a big tree whose trunk was so wide it must have been there since the beginning of time. They dismounted the horses, and the Being, that appeared to be of light, spoke to the young man.

"You have come thus far thanks to your pure mind that is calm and free of fear. And thanks to your noble heart that is filled with reverence for this forest. It carries within marvelous secrets, some of which you may come to know. But we must also inform you that when it is time for you to leave, you will not remember anything you have seen.

You will carry with you your inner transformation, and all you will be able to tell is that the forest is magical indeed.

"This is done to protect the sanctity of the forest, for only to a few chosen ones does the forest reveal its true nature. You have been tested in several ways, without you being aware of it. Many people have approached the forest with knives or other devices, prepared to defend themselves by hurting the living creatures. They have approached the forest with fear and aggression in their minds. When the forest perceives this, it refrains from manifesting its marvels.

"When the bear approached you, he felt you meant no harm. He was grateful for that, respected you, and continued his way. I must tell you again you will forget everything you see. Do you wish to continue?"

"Yes," answered the young man, filled with gratitude toward this magnificent forest and its beautiful Being.

The Being placed the palm of his hand on the trunk of the tree. Before the young man's eyes, part of the trunk started to dematerialize, revealing an arched entryway.

He entered and signaled for the young man to follow. They went inside the trunk, into a small chamber with transparent walls. As soon as they were both inside, the chamber started to descend, gliding downward as if going into the center of the earth.

When it stopped, the doorway opened and they found themselves in a beautiful cave with an amber light, glowing as if coming from the rock itself. They stepped out from the cave and the young man could not believe his eyes. A forest within the forest!

Every particle in nature seemed to be radiating its own light. A soft, yellow light illuminated the sky, and right beside them was the most beautiful lake.

The Being addressed the young man. "Go into the water and stay there a while. The lake will regenerate every cell of your being. Your body will be youthful and forever healthy."

The young man immersed himself in the lake. He could feel the coolness of the water, yet strangely, his body did not get wet. It was a soothing feeling, relaxing his entire body. He let himself drift in this miraculous water, looking at the glow in the sky, feeling in absolute harmony with himself and with nature. Time seemed to stand still, until he heard the voice of the Being, asking him to step outside. Then he spoke again.

"There are energy bands which protect our world and no visitor is able to penetrate them on their own. You have been invited here to help protect the sanctity of the forest in your world. Even if by the end of your journey here you will not remember what you have seen, you will know the forest to be a sacred place, and you will help maintain it that way.

"Our time together is coming to an end," the Being continued. "I will now escort you back to your world."

The young man's heart was overflowing with love and gratitude. He felt sad that he had to leave, but at the same time, he knew that his life was being transformed in a way no words could explain.

In a moment's time, they found themselves back where the young man had left his satchel. He picked it up, ready to go back home. But before parting, he asked, "How can I ever thank you?"

And one last time, the Being spoke. "This forest has nourished you. For the next six days, you won't need any food. You will be protected; no harm will come your way. It is we who are grateful to you for living your life with integrity and reverence for all living creatures on earth." With these words, the Being disappeared.

The young man started his journey back home, and when he arrived after six days, all he could tell was that the forest was a magical place indeed.

The Magician

*O*nce upon a time, in a far and remote kingdom, there was a castle in the middle of a beautiful lake. On the grounds were the most exotic plants, and peacocks walked in its gardens. The lake was of a translucent deep blue, and if one looked closely, one could see the shimmering colors of the many fish that lived within it.

In the castle, there lived a king and queen with their beautiful daughter. The king loved his people and ruled his kingdom righteously, while the queen and their daughter took great care of the many festivities that were offered throughout the year. Many times, they would stroll in the gardens together, and it was often during those moments that they would plan their upcoming events.

It was on one of those days that they were planning a very special feast, one that was very dear to their hearts. Everyone in the kingdom spoke of a magician who had extraordinary powers. Nobody had seen him, or even knew where he lived.

But one night, the queen had a dream in which the magician appeared to her and asked her to prepare a banquet where her and the king, together with their daughter and sixteen chosen guests, were to be present. He said it would be an occasion where everyone attending would receive a profound teaching. In her dream, the queen asked how she would know how to contact him, but the magician just smiled and said, "Let this be of no concern to you. I will take care of it." With this, the dream ended.

When the queen awoke the next morning, she immediately told her husband and daughter about it. They were all puzzled. Nonetheless, they were eager to plan for this mysterious event because deep in their hearts they knew that they were to receive a very special blessing.

Carefully and with great attention, they started to prepare for this gathering. All sixteen guests were chosen. They were to be seated around a superbly decorated table filled with the finest delicacies. Candles and flowers abundantly decorated the room and the atmosphere was one of excitement mixed with reverence. One by one the guests arrived. When everyone was present, the king and queen thanked them for coming, and then introduced their daughter, a princess with exquisite features, who had grown into a beautiful young woman.

As the last guest was invited to take his seat at the table, they all noticed that one chair had remained empty. It was reserved for the guest of honor, a being no one had ever seen but everyone had heard of. The great magician.

All the guests were waiting with anticipation when suddenly there was a knock at the door, and after a few moments, the magician entered the room. He was impeccably dressed; his clothes made of a material no one had ever seen before. The guests could not discern if it was made of fabric or of light.

He greeted the king, the queen, the princess, and each of the guests. Then he sat on the empty chair.

A sumptuous meal was served and all the guests felt superbly entertained. But the magician kept very quiet. At the end of the lavish meal, he stood up and spoke. "I thank you for having invited me tonight. In appreciation, I have brought you two very rare gifts: one for the queen and one for the princess."

He placed on the table two beautiful and ornate bottles that appeared to be identical. He then continued. "One of these bottles carries an elixir that endows one's body with eternal youth. The other bottle comes with an elixir as well. When drunk, one's spirit will remain eternally young." Then he addressed the queen and the princess. "I will let each one of you choose the bottle which you desire the most."

The queen, who was starting to worry about the first signs of her body aging, immediately said, "I would like my body to be eternally young."

But the princess, who was born with a great and noble heart, said, "I am so grateful for your gift, oh Master. A young, light spirit is the greatest treasure I can wish for. I thank you greatly."

The magician nodded and said, "Very well. I honor your wishes. Your desires will be fulfilled. There are no mistakes in life. Whatever you wish for is what you will receive. "With these words, he handed one bottle to the queen and one to the princess.

The magician watched them closely as they both drank the elixir at the same time. He then tapped strongly on the table and the whole room, with everyone in it, was enveloped by a golden light.

All the guests sitting around the table saw themselves in the same setting, forty years into the future. They all looked at the queen and the princess. The queen's body did not present any signs of age, but somehow she did not look young. As they turned to look at the princess, they noticed that she had a few signs of aging and lifelines adorned her face. *But what was it?* the guests wondered. In spite of the lines on her face, the princess looked much younger than the queen, whose skin was as smooth as a child's.

While the guests were still wondering at the contradiction, the magician spoke again. "The human body is a translucent garment that clothes the spirit. Even if you are blessed with a beautiful body, if your spirit is heavy, you will never look young. In the same way, if your body ages naturally and you can maintain a light and youthful spirit, you will never look old."

Once again, the magician tapped strongly on the table, and they were all brought back forty years to the present, to that splendid evening meal. All the guests looked at each other and then looked at the chair where the magician had sat. He was no longer there. No one said a word. They were all thinking about one phrase the magician had said. "The human body is a translucent garment that clothes the spirit."

That night, at the table, each one understood the magnificence of their own being. Each one understood the importance of living with a light heart and a young spirit.

The Alchemist

*O*nce upon a time, there was a village renowned for one man. Many people traveled for days and weeks to come and see this man, as they were all hoping to learn from him. He was the great alchemist who transmuted base metal into gold.

Yet he was very peculiar. In spite of all the riches he could possibly make, he lived modestly and, what seemed to most people, in great poverty. His only possessions were a small hut where he lived with a young boy, and his camel. When people would come to see him, often they would find him sitting in silence in the back of his hut, watching the young boy take care of the camel.

People came from all walks of life, rich and poor alike. They all wanted to learn his secret. As they came in front of the old man, one by one, he would watch them carefully. He was able to perceive their true intentions. He knew they all came to learn how to enrich themselves with material possessions. Then he would tell them, "To understand my secret, you just have to polish."

At that point, he usually would get up and walk back into his hut, leaving the astonished people with their own thoughts. They all left, wondering about this strange man, and did not know what to make of his answer. They were disappointed, as they felt they were not receiving the secret at all; for all of them had heard great stories about this man who could transform base metal into gold.

But only the alchemist knew that there are wonderful experiences that no gold can buy. These are the true treasures that would enrich and transform everyone's life beyond imagination.

In the meantime, the alchemist kept watching his young boy. He was noble at heart, pure in mind, and loved the camel with all his heart. During the day, he would clean and feed it, and then he would take it out for a ride. At night, he would get his blanket and lie beside the camel, his head resting on the soft belly of the animal. Before drifting into sleep, the boy would watch the stars above him, and gratitude filled his heart. Nothing made him happier than taking care of the camel, that he felt had become his best and most loyal friend over the years. He would listen to the camel's breath and feel its body rise and fall. And happily, he would close his eyes, knowing that everything was well.

One morning the alchemist called upon the boy and said, "I have been waiting all these years for you to grow and learn what I have to teach you. Now you are ready to learn true alchemy."

The boy, who was now a young man, instinctively felt that he had come to the alchemist to receive something marvelous.

The master continued. "To turn base metal into gold, you must polish." Then he handed him a metal rod and a piece of cloth.

The boy did not question the old man's words, so he started polishing, happy that the alchemist would share his secret with him. He polished for many days, but nothing happened.

Seeing that, the boy went to his master to find out if he was doing everything the right way, but the alchemist replied, "First, you must polish your mind and your heart, then you polish the metal."

With this, he dismissed the boy, telling him, "You are free to go for the rest of the day. Think about what I have told you."

The boy went off and thought long about his own mind. What was there to polish? What did he have to achieve? What was his master trying to tell him?

As he did not know what to do, he came back to the master's camel, and together they went for a long ride in silence, the boy pondering the alchemist's words.

Days, weeks, and months went by in this way. Slowly, the youngster's mind started to become more focused. He was becoming self-aware of his own thoughts. Instead of his mind wandering away on its own, he was learning to gently guide it to where he wanted it to go. By doing this, he started to realize that he was not his mind, or his emotions. Slowly, he began to feel that there was something more magnificent inside of him that was beginning to manifest.

On one of the mornings when he went to see the alchemist, something peculiar happened. He was taking the rod that his master had given him to polish, in the same way he had done all these past months. But to his surprise, the metal started changing its color ever so slightly. Excited, he showed it to his master, but all he said to the boy was "Keep polishing. You are headed in the right direction."

Many more days and weeks went by.

The lad kept taking care of his beloved camel, he kept polishing his rod, and he continued his long rides in silence, contemplating his own mind.

He was able to see how his mind was ever so closely connected to his emotions. But now, they did not affect him, as he had learned to guide his mind in the right direction. He had become a master of his own mind.

This gave him great peace and he started experiencing immense joy and happiness inside of himself. His mind had become calm and serene. This let him focus on his inner self, and the more he did that, the more love he felt in his heart.

As time went by, his whole appearance started to change; one could see a light shining from his eyes that transformed his whole being.

One afternoon, as he was polishing the metal rod, to his amazement, he saw that it had turned into pure gold. Humbly, he took it to his master, handing it to him without saying a word.

The master's heart overflowed with love for his boy. He knew that he had understood the secret that so many people failed to recognize. With great affection, he looked deep into the young man's eyes and said, "You have learned true alchemy, for your entire being is glowing with light. Everything you come in contact with will be filled with golden light. This is what I had to teach you, and this is more precious than all the gold on earth. Because of your dedication and patience, you developed a love that is far more significant than all earthly possessions. You have learned to treasure and protect this love, and nobody will ever take this away from you. Each person is like a jewel that needs to be polished for the light and the love of God to shine through. Now you will be able to handle any situation in life, no matter how difficult or challenging, with the utmost love, serenity, and joy in your heart."

From that day on, the alchemist was not seen anymore. The young man would sit behind the hut, taking care of his camel, and when people came to see him and ask him about his secret, he would say, "All you have to do is polish." And with this, he would get up and disappear inside the hut.

The Sacred Union

*O*nce upon a time, in a land far away, there was a kingdom ruled by a king and queen endowed with great hearts who looked after their people, leading them into prosperous lives. They were greatly loved by everyone.

One fine morning, they called together all their people and announced that they were going to have a baby. Everyone in the kingdom was overjoyed, and as time went by, a baby girl was born.

The villagers brought the finest gifts they could offer to their king and queen, and everyone was happy and filled with gratitude. They were eager to see the baby grow and watched her fondly whenever her parents would show her publicly.

It was one late afternoon, at sunset, that the arrival of the Great Wise One was announced. He was highly respected by everyone, and many times people would come to him, asking all kinds of questions. But he never answered when asked. He only spoke when he considered it necessary. When the king and queen heard that he had asked to be seen by them, they were highly honored.

His presence radiated pure light when he addressed them privately. "You have been blessed with the birth of a beautiful soul. This soul has been the chosen one. One day, she will be united with the Master of all Masters. I pay homage to this great light." He placed his hand above the child's forehead and, without further words, left.

The king and queen were puzzled, for they did not understand what he meant, so they decided not to say anything to anyone about what was revealed to them in secret.

Time went by and the baby grew into a beautiful girl who was the only heir to the throne.

When she came of age, the king and queen started considering which young man could be offered to their child as a groom. But the princess seemed to have no interest in anyone. She liked to be very much by herself, in the company of nature and her dear animal friends.

Every evening she would stroll in the magnificent gardens of the palace. The king and queen would hear the most melodious and enchanting songs through the open window that would slowly fade away as their daughter would reach her favorite place: the palace's lake.

It was a beautiful lake surrounded by trees and flowers, and it was here where the princess communed with nature.

She would sing every night to her angel, sensing his presence with her. Two deer with their fawns would come regularly and lie by her side. She then would grow very quiet and attune herself to the energy of nature: the plants, the animals, the flowers, and the lake. It was those moments she held so dear to her heart. She treasured them more than anything else.

In the meantime, the king and queen continued thinking about which possible suitors they could introduce to their daughter. Carefully, and with much love, they started to plan a feast with guests from near and far.

The appointed time came, and everyone in the palace started preparing themselves for this important event. There was excitement in the air, for the king had invited a few young men of royal birth, hoping their daughter would find the right groom.

The princess gracefully adorned herself, though mostly to please her parents who had no idea about the secret she treasured so much, for her heart was already taken.

She attended the feast in the company of her parents and was introduced to several young men. As the night came to an end, each of the guests paid their respects to the royal family and prepared to leave. The king and queen looked inquiringly at their dear daughter. But when they saw the look in her eyes, they understood they had not succeeded in finding her love.

It was then that the princess spoke to her mother and father. "I am so grateful and touched by your efforts in trying to find me someone I can marry. I realize that you have great hope in me to someday start a family of my own. My dear father and mother, this I must say to you: I have found indeed my true love and my heart is already taken. He is present in my dreams, and is with me every minute of the day. He is my protector and the only one who can set me free."

The king and queen looked at each other, not quite understanding what their daughter meant.

"The day is approaching when I will be finally united with my dear One."

The king and queen did not know whether to be happy or sad. They were glad to see their daughter so in love and filled with joy, and at the same time, they were sensing that she would be leaving soon. They sat confused, looking at their beautiful child, when suddenly they remembered the Great Wise One's last words. "She will be united with the Master of all Masters."

At that moment, the king and queen were greatly humbled and realized the immense honor that their child's destiny would represent. They said to their beloved daughter, "We are so very happy for you, for now we realize you are living a blessed life." They embraced each other, and warm feelings of love filled all of their hearts.

The princess kept going to the lake whenever she could, and there she would immerse herself with the spirit of nature. In this way, many months passed.

One day, it was late in the evening when the princess went to her parents and said, "My dear father and mother, it will happen the next moon cycle, on the night when the moon is full. You have been asked to come with me to the lake." The king's and queen's hearts were being carefully protected by beings of light, so sadness would not overwhelm them. They knew they were about to witness something very special at their daughter's departure.

At the appointed time, on the night of the full moon, the princess and her parents started walking toward the lake. When they arrived, they saw, rising from the ground, a soaring violet-blue flame and, standing beside it, a messenger of light of immense beauty. He addressed the royal family. "I salute each one of you with reverence."

Then he turned to the king and queen and said, "On this very auspicious night, your daughter will be entering a gateway into another dimension. She will be prepared for the sacred union with the Master of all Masters. You will be blessed with a heart full of joy for the duration of your lives."

Then he looked at the princess and asked her, "Are you ready?"

She nodded.

"We will enter this sacred flame, which you will find cool to the touch. This is the gateway."

She embraced her father and mother and was happy not to perceive any trace of sadness in their hearts.

The messenger entered the flame and the princess followed. She turned around to look once more at her parents, raised her hand, and from her palm a ray of light and energy enveloped them with pure love. At that moment, the flame disappeared.

The princess found herself following the messenger into an ample corridor that was ornate with exquisite designs and crystals. She had never seen something so beautiful. They entered an archway and the messenger opened a door leading to a chamber. Inside was a basin filled with a translucent golden-yellow substance.

The messenger said to the princess, "You are to take a bath and rest there for a while. When you are ready, I will knock on the door and wait outside. Do you have any questions?"

The princess nodded. "I don't see anything to cleanse my body with."

The messenger replied, "The bath is not for your body. It is for your soul."

"How will you know when I am ready?" the princess asked.

"Don't worry," he answered gently. "I will know." With those words, he walked out the door.

The princess removed her clothes and carefully stepped inside the golden liquid.

Suddenly, she started hearing the most melodious music and began feeling a torrent of love pour from her heart. She lay in this way for some time, and unexpectedly, all her previous lifetimes started flashing before her eyes. She saw herself sometimes as a man and sometimes as a woman. She was able to see in all her lifetimes a deep love and longing for something she could not find in her life on earth.

She had been very much on her own, lifetime after lifetime learning lessons that evolved her spirit, each lifetime leading into new growth. She became witness to all the suffering the separation from the Invisible had caused, and tears started to roll down her cheeks. It felt her soul was being cleansed after countless lifetimes.

When she had seen all her lives pass by, her mind grew calm and an outpour of love permeated her whole being.

She remained for a while in this state, and then slowly she got up. Her body was not wet at all and when she looked, she was clothed in the most beautiful garments that shined as if made by light. She noticed her body becoming ethereal.

Suddenly, she heard the knock on the door. It was the messenger. She stepped outside and knew she was to follow him.

They walked through the ample corridor that was flanked on both sides by beings of light, all looking kindly and lovingly at her. Out of their hands came particles that seemed to be glitters of light falling gently over her. The messenger told her, "All the beings are sending you their blessings."

At this moment, the messenger stepped aside. At the very end of the hallway, the princess could barely see a figure. It was enveloped by pure light.

Beautiful music was heard in the air, and very slowly, she started walking toward the Being of light. Each step she took, she could feel her love growing stronger and stronger, and as she reached her destination, she recognized her Master, her Angel and Protector. The light had become so strong she could no more see her surroundings. An immense longing filled her heart, and at this moment, the Being of light enveloped her and they became one luminous, radiant presence.

This presence forever shined in the sky and it became by far the largest and brightest star in the firmament. It blessed all people in the kingdom and throughout all corners of the earth.

Each time someone would look at this star, they could feel pure love radiating from it and filling their lives with happiness and hope. And if they faced difficulties at times, it renewed their faith. People came to understand that, whatever struggle they were going through, it was necessary and worth it, in order for their souls to grow.

About the Author

Patrizia was born in 1967 as the first of three children into a loving family of five. Her light-heartedness and carefree demeanor as a young girl provided that special bond that ties a family together. She was a daily reminder to her parents and siblings of all that is wondrous and pure.

Of European descent but raised in South America, she was well-traveled and cultured by the time she was a teenager. But deep inside her lay a yearning to explore the *internal* vastness and beauty of the human experience. And so it was only natural that she would follow a path of spirituality during those restless and inquisitive teenage years.

Patrizia matured into a special, albeit reserved, young woman. Knowing that many times it is the ego that tarnishes an individual's soul and that karma is a universal law to which we are all bound, she was incapable of seeing any bad or negative qualities in people—a realization that comes only to those with a deep spiritual understanding.

But not only did she see the good in people; she also always made a special effort to make everyone she met *feel* good about themselves. Now more than ever, Patrizia's soul was bursting with radiant light.

Her stoic attitude was unshaken when she was diagnosed with breast cancer in her late thirties. At 44, she was given just six months to live, but she brushed aside the evidence as inconvenient and for three more years kept volunteering her time to benefit others. Never once did she lament her fate or complain about pain. Quite the contrary, she became stronger and an even greater example of how to accept those events that render our lives difficult. She passed away peacefully, surrounded by her family, in the summer of 2014, embracing the reality of transcending to a higher state of being.